WHEN THE STORM COMES

written by
LINDA ASHMAN

illustrated by
TAEEUN YOO

 Nancy Paulsen Books

Nancy Paulsen Books
An imprint of Penguin Random House LLC, New York

Text copyright © 2020 by Linda Ashman | Illustrations copyright © 2020 by Taeeun Yoo

Nancy Paulsen Books is a trademark of Penguin Random House LLC.

Visit us online at penguinrandomhouse.com

Library of Congress Cataloging-in-Publication Data | Names: Ashman, Linda, author. | Yoo, Taeeun, illustrator.
Title: When the storm comes / Linda Ashman; illustrated by Taeeun Yoo. | Description: New York: Nancy Paulsen Books, [2020] |
Summary: Illustrations and easy-to-read, rhyming text show the many different ways in which people and animals prepare for a storm
and take shelter. | Identifiers: LCCN 2019018213 | ISBN 9780399546099 (hardcover: alk. paper) | ISBN 9780399546129 (ebook) |
ISBN 9780399546105 (ebook) | Subjects: | CYAC: Stories in rhyme. | Storms—Fiction. | Animals—Fiction. |
Classification: LCC PZ8.3.A775 Whk 2020 | DDC [E]—dc23 | LC record available at https://lccn.loc.gov/2019018213
Manufactured in China by RR Donnelley Asia Printing Solutions Ltd.
ISBN 9780399546099
Special Markets ISBN 9780593354681 Not for Resale
10 9 8 7 6 5 4 3 2 1
Design by Eileen Savage and Nicole Rheingans | Text set in Calvert MT Pro
The illustrations were created using digital and pencil drawing.

This Imagination Library edition is published by Penguin Young Readers, a division
of Penguin Random House, exclusively for Dolly Parton's Imagination Library,
a not-for-profit program designed to inspire a love of reading and learning, sponsored
in part by The Dollywood Foundation. Penguin's trade editions of this work are
available wherever books are sold.

For Judy, friend extraordinaire,
who weathers every storm
with strength and grace —L.A.

For my family, with love —T.Y.

What do you do when the clouds roll in,
When the wind chimes clang and the weather vanes spin?

We watch.

We sniff.

We perk our ears,

And listen as the rumbling nears.

We count supplies.

We check the news.

We find our comfort spot.

We s n o o z e.

Where do you go when the sky turns gray—
When the grasses bend and the treetops sway?

We gather here below the eaves.

We roost beneath some sturdy leaves.

We put our busywork aside,
And buzz back to the hive to hide.

We find a small, protected space—
A hollow log, a sheltered place.

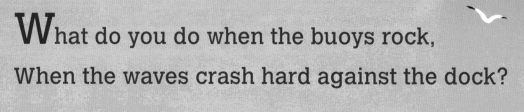

What do you do when the buoys rock,

When the waves crash hard against the dock?

We ride a blast of stormy air.

We find a cove—it's safer there.

We dodge the weather, if we can—
We swim down deep, away from land.

We close. We cover,
Latch and tie.

We bring things in
To keep them dry.

Then lightning cracks,
And thunder ROARS—
It shakes the shutters, rattles doors.
The rain pours down.
The sky turns slate . . .

We hunker down to watch and wait.

We play a game by candlelight,
Tell some stories,
Curl up tight.

We listen to the rainfall rush—

Then . . .

Drizzle . . .

Patter . . .

Plip . . .

Plop . . .

Hush.

What do you do when the storm has passed—
When the sun comes out and it's calm at last?

We leave our dens.

We scout.

We fly.

We shake, shake, shake until we're dry.

We clean things up.

We sweep and rake.

We haul debris.

We mix and bake.

We check on neighbors.

Make repairs.

Bring out tables.

Pull up chairs.

We settle in, enjoy the sun,

Happy that the storm is done.

Grateful for the change in weather—

And for friends who flock together.